Delicious and Nutritious

The Prince of Picky Eating Tries New Foods

ISBN: 978-1-7361873-4-0 (Paperback)
ISBN: 978-1-7361873-5-7 (Hardcover)
ISBN: 978-1-7361873-6-4 (E-book)

Illustrations by: Mariana Hnatenko of Nimble Pencils

First printing edition 2021.

Melanated Magic Books

www.staceywoodson.com

For my children, your existence is
my inspiration.

– SW

This is Stanton. He is sweet, sophisticated, and super smart.

However, he has a simply silly story!

Stanton is particular and picky, especially when it comes to food! He only eats foods that begin with the letter B. Some of these foods are nutritious but it has become a problem because there are so many foods he will not eat. Although Stanton is sophisticated and super smart, he is also seriously stubborn.

Each day Stanton's mother explains how important it is to eat foods from all the different food groups – **fruits, vegetables (veggies), grains, protein, dairy, and fat**. Each of these food groups offers different **vitamins** and **minerals**, which are necessary to help you stay healthy and grow strong.

Stanton's family became **vegetarian** (which means they do not eat meat) a few years ago. This was after Stanton refused to eat anything except beans, butter, and blue corn chips. Now he also eats bananas, bread, and broccoli (only if it's blanched) – but that's it! Stanton's mom has had it! She is frazzled, frustrated, and furious by his finicky eating habits.

Stanton's mother says, "There are lots of foods that are delicious and nutritious!" Stanton is uninterested.

During snack time, Stanton's mom explains that **protein** helps your muscles grow big and strong. "This is **hummus**, it is made with **chickpeas**. It is a very popular food in many Middle Eastern countries. I choose hummus as a snack because it contains protein and **fiber** which help you feel full longer. I think you will like it. It is delicious and nutritious," explains Stanton's mom. Stanton stared at the plate and stated, "No, thank you! Not today! No way!"

"Tonight is try something new Tuesday," explained Stanton's dad, "We are having **quinoa** and **kale**! People in South America commonly eat quinoa. In the United States, we consider it a part of the **grain** food group as many people eat quinoa instead of rice. However, it's really an **edible** seed! It is a good source of protein and rich in minerals such as **Manganese** which has several necessary functions in the body."

Stanton was annoyed, aggravated, and appalled. His parents actually thought he would eat quinoa! However, he smiled and softly stated, "No, thank you! Not today! No way!"

Stanton loves playing at his friend Kamon's house. He has all the best toys! Unfortunately, Kamon's mom always tries to offer Stanton something to eat during their playdates and today was no different! Stanton desperately tried to dash out of the door before snack time.

That definitely didn't happen! Kamon's mom exclaimed, "This is **dragon fruit**; it may look odd but it's sweet and really good for you. It is rich in **antioxidants** – substances that protect cells and keep them healthy. I used to eat it all the time growing up in Thailand. I think you will like it!" Stanton says, "Let me guess, it's delicious and nutritious?" "Yes! How did you know?" asked Kamon's mom. Stanton chuckled, "It's just a guess!" He didn't want to be rude, so in his most polite voice, he said, "No, thank you. Not today. No way."

"Look at this **callaloo** growing in the garden, it is so green and gorgeous!" Stanton's mom announced, "People in several Caribbean countries grow and eat callaloo. In Jamaica, it is prepared like greens and cooked with tomatoes, peppers, and spices. It's a great source of many vitamins such as **vitamin A** which is important for healthy vision. I think you would like it! It's delicious and nutritious!"

Stanton shook his head and said, "No, thank you. Not today. No way."

"What kind of snacks would you like to eat this week?" asked Stanton's mom. Paige, Stanton's sister, passionately pleaded for peach yogurt!

"Great idea! Yogurt is a great source of **calcium** and **probiotics**. Calcium is important for strong bones and teeth. Probiotics are important for healthy **digestion**. Let's try something new, pick out some **non-dairy** yogurts. This yogurt made with coconut milk looks yummy!" said Stanton's mom. Paige looks at Stanton and mimics their mom, "I think you will like it! It's delicious and nutritious!" Stanton was still skeptical, he says "No, thank you. Not today. No way."

shopping list

bananas
cans of beans
bread
broccoli
hummus
carrots
guacamole
bag of avocados
dragon fruit
quinoa
kale
cucumbers

Later that night as Stanton and Paige were putting away groceries, they acted goofy while they gabbed about Stanton's recent birthday celebration. Stanton received some really cool gifts. However, he would not let Paige look at them, let alone play with his new toys. Paige suddenly came up with a sneaky scenario to play with the new toys. She decided to challenge Stanton to a dare.

Paige absolutely adored avocados, and she knew Stanton didn't like to try new things. Paige decided to dare Stanton to try avocados. If Stanton refused the dare, Paige would get to play with Stanton's new toys!

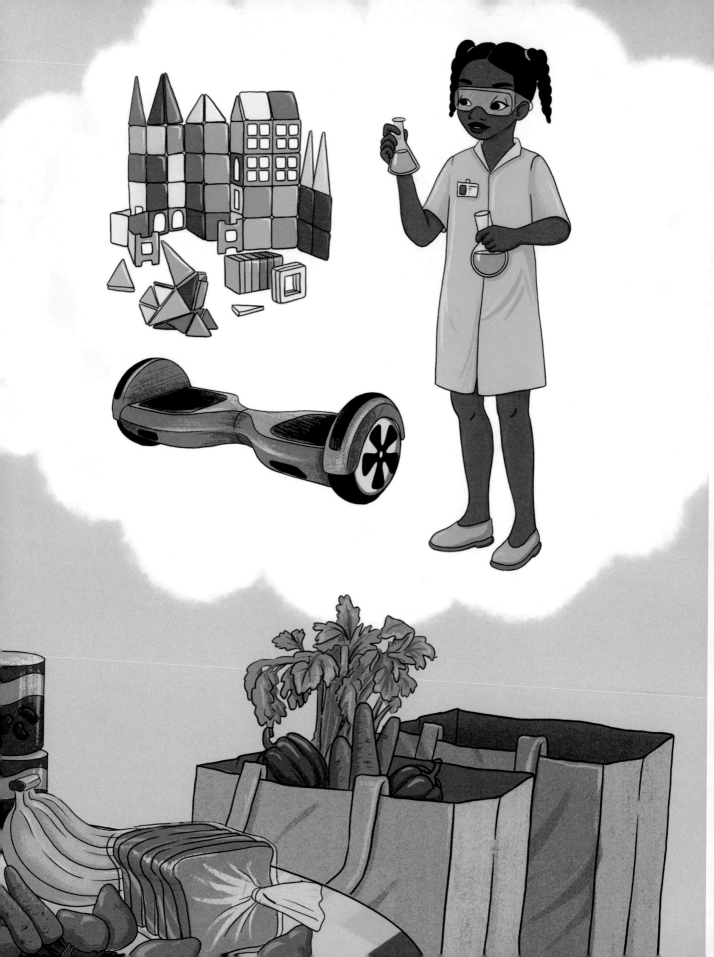

Now remember Stanton is sweet – yet sophisticated and super smart, so he was clear this was not a good deal. Stanton said, "If I try avocados and I don't like them you can play with my toys. If I try them and I do like them, you have to do my chores for one week. Deal?" Paige agreed, after all, Stanton does not eat anything except for foods that begin with the letter B.

Stanton snickered as he had a surprise for Paige. Once a few years ago, while Stanton was distracted, their mom had secretly served him a spoonful of **guacamole** - a dip made with avocados.

He remembered his mother explaining how avocados are often grown in Mexico. They are really nutritious because they contain healthy fats called **monounsaturated fatty acids** that are good for your heart. Stanton was pretty sure he could pretend to enjoy avocados... in the form of guacamole to win the dare.

As his family watched, Stanton brilliantly and boldly grabbed some guacamole and took a bite...

Time stood still as he tasted the tortilla chip topped with guacamole. Paige earnestly, eagerly, and emotionally awaited his response. Stanton slowly states, "I think I like it...Actually, it's amazing! I would eat it any day! I would eat avocados any way! It is delicious and nutritious!"

Stanton's family was staring silently and stunned. He had single-handedly won the dare! Stanton was so surprised by his new discovery he decided to try other new foods.

Over the course of the next few days, he happily tried hummus and thought it was heavenly. Next, he quietly sampled quinoa and quickly admitted it was quite enjoyable.

Afterward, Stanton daringly dined on dragon fruit, dazzled and delighted by the sweet delectable flavor. Next, he curiously chewed the callaloo and was captivated by the flavorful food. Last, he yelled "yummy" after tasting the smooth and creamy texture of yogurt.

Stanton was finally fully aware that trying new foods could be fun! It was also DELICIOUS and NUTRITIOUS!!!

He was so proud of himself! He was also happy that Paige dared him to try something new! He was so happy that he even let Paige play with his new toys!

Glossary

Antioxidants - Substances that help cells in the body stay healthy by protecting them from being damaged.

Calcium - A silver-white mineral found in teeth and bones, which is necessary for many chemical processes in the human body.

Callaloo - The large edible leaves of a tropical plant, widely used in Caribbean cooking.

Chickpeas - The edible seed of a plant originally grown in Asia. Also called garbanzo beans.

Dairy food group - A group of foods made with cow's milk. Foods in the dairy group include milk, yogurt, cheese, and ice cream.

Digestion - The process of breaking down food and separating from it the things that the body needs.

Dragon fruit - A large usually oval to oblong fruit in the cactus family.

Edible - Able to be eaten.

Fat food group - Fats are used to make nerve tissue, hormones, and energy. Fats are found in foods such as meat, milk, cheese, nuts, and avocados.

Fiber - A part of fruits, vegetables, and grains that passes through the body but is not digested. Fiber helps food move through the intestines.

Fruit food group - The fleshy, juicy product of a plant that contains one or more seeds.

Grain food group - Seed or fruit of a grain plant. Grains include cereals such as barley, oats, wheat, and rye.

Guacamole - A dip made of avocado, onions, lime juice, and seasonings.

Hummus - A dip or sandwich spread made of chickpeas and sesame paste.

Kale - A green leafy vegetable in the same family as cabbage and broccoli. It is often eaten raw and cooked.

Manganese - A grayish-white mineral responsible for many functions including bone building, wound healing, and metabolism of carbohydrates and amino acids.

Minerals - A solid substance found in the earth that is not made by animals or plants. Your body needs vitamins and minerals to stay healthy.

Monounsaturated Fatty Acids (MUFA) - A type of fat needed for a healthy heart and cholesterol levels. Found in foods such as olive oil, nuts, and avocados.

Non-dairy - A term used for dairy products created without cow's milk. Alternative milks such as soy, almond, coconut, hemp, oat, etc. are used to create non-dairy products.

Probiotics - Living microorganisms (usually bacteria) that are similar to good microorganisms found in the digestive tract. They are found in certain foods or are taken as dietary supplements. They are useful for healthy digestion.

Protein food group - Protein is needed to build and maintain muscles, bone, and skin. Foods such as meat, cheese, eggs, beans, fish, and soy are sources of protein.

Quinoa - The seed of a South American plant that is cooked and eaten for food.

Vegetables (veggies) food group - A plant or part of a plant used as food, which is rich in vitamins, minerals, and fiber. Vegetables are usually eaten as side dishes or in salads.

Vegetarian - A person who only eats plants and plant products and sometimes eggs or dairy products.

Vitamin - An essential micronutrient that is necessary in small quantities for normal health and growth. Vitamins are obtained from the food people eat.

Vitamin A - An essential vitamin needed for many functions including growth and development, vision, and immune function.

About the Author:

Stacey Woodson, MS, RD, LDN is a dietitian-nutritionist and entrepreneur. She is a counselor, speaker, and author on the topics of nutrition and wellness.

She loves teaching children about healthy eating and introducing them to new foods. She also has a passion for representing and affirming children of color which inspired her to start a clothing line named Melanated Magic Tees. Stacey enjoys gardening, foraging, yoga, and spending time in nature. Delicious and Nutritious: The Prince of Picky Eating Tries New Foods is the second book in her series. It was inspired by and loosely based on her children. Stacey lives in Philadelphia, PA with her husband, three children, and her cat.

Find Stacey at www.staceywoodson.com

Made in the USA
Coppell, TX
16 November 2021

65865397R00024